BEAR'S
BICYCLE

FOR JOE

Text copyright © 2021 Laura Renauld
Illustrations copyright © 2021 Beaming Books

Published in 2021 by Beaming Books, an imprint of 1517 Media.
All rights reserved. No part of this book may be reproduced
without the written permission of the publisher.
Email copyright@1517.media.
Printed in Canada.

27 26 25 24 23 22 21   1 2 3 4 5 6 7 8

Hardcover ISBN: 978-1-5064-6569-2
Ebook ISBN: 978-1-5064-6950-8

Library of Congress Cataloging-in-Publication Data
Names: Renauld, Laura, author. | Poh, Jennie, illustrator.
Title: Bear's bicycle / by Laura Renauld ; illustrated by Jennie Poh.
Description: Minneapolis, MN : Beaming Books, 2021. | Audience: Ages 3-8. |
Summary: When Bear struggles to get the hang of riding his bike, his
friends are there to support him by practicing together and cheering him
on as he learns a new skill. Includes bike safety tips.
Identifiers: LCCN 2020028841 (print) | LCCN 2020028842 (ebook) | ISBN
9781506465692 (hardcover) | ISBN 9781506469508 (ebook)
Subjects: CYAC: Bears--Fiction. | Bicycles and bicycling--Fiction. |
Friendship--Fiction.
Classification: LCC PZ7.1.R463 Be 2021 (print) | LCC PZ7.1.R463 (ebook) |
DDC ⟨E⟩--dc23
LC record available at https://lccn.loc.gov/2020028841
LC ebook record available at https://lccn.loc.gov/2020028842

VN0004589; 9781506465692; FEB2021

Beaming Books
510 Marquette Avenue
Minneapolis, MN 55402
Beamingbooks.com

BEAR'S BICYCLE

BY LAURA RENAULD

ILLUSTRATED BY JENNIE POH

beaming books

MINNEAPOLIS

Summer Scoot was just around the corner,
and Bear was doing everything by the book.

Tighten. Grease. *Ring.* Pump. Strap. Shine.
Finally, Bear's bicycle was ready.

He opened *Learn to Ride in Five Easy Steps*:

1. Straddle

"Easy," said Bear.

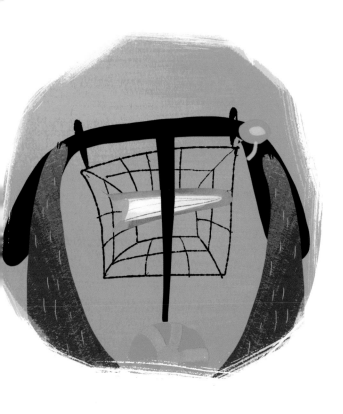

2. Grip

Bear clenched the handlebars.
He planted himself on the seat
and prepared his feet.

3. Pedal

Bear pushed off and . . .

4. Balance

Pedal-wibble. Pedal-wobble. Crash!

"Ouch!" said Bear. "That wasn't easy at all. I need a different book." Bear brushed himself off and walked down the path with his bicycle.

On his way to the library, Bear ran into Porcupine.
"Hello, Bear! I didn't see you there."

"Hello, Porcupine. It looks like
you're ready for Summer Scoot!"

"I sure am," said Porcupine, noticing the book
in Bear's basket. "Step five is my favorite!"
She grinned, then sped away.

"I didn't even get that far," Bear said with a sigh.

As Bear continued down the path, he saw Doe in the distance. Her riding was smooth, then jolty. Straight, then swervy. Balanced, then leaning, then . . . *oof!*

Doe sighed.
"I'm glad you're here, Bear.
I don't feel ready for Summer Scoot."

"Riding a bicycle is hard. That's why
I'm going to the library for a new book,"
said Bear. "We can go together."

Doe rode down the path.
Bear provided encouragement.

"You're doing great!"

"Keep it steady."

"Don't forget to pedal."

When they arrived at
the library, Doe smiled.
"Thank you, Bear.
You're a good friend."

"Watch out!" a familiar voice shouted.

Pedal-wibble. Pedal-wobble. Crash!

"Sorry, Bear," said Squirrel.
"Sometimes I forget how to stop."

Bear watched Squirrel
jump back on her bike.
"Squirrel, are you ready
for Summer Scoot?"

"Not yet, but I'm working on it!"

Bear looked at his friends and thought,
Porcupine likes to practice,
Doe rides better when a friend is with her,
and Squirrel never gives up.

Bear straddled his bicycle.
"Maybe I don't need another book," he said.
"Maybe I just need to try again . . ."

". . . and again . . . ," said Bear.

". . . with a friend."

Bear grinned. "Summer Scoot, here we come!"

HOW TO CARE FOR YOUR TWO-WHEELER
BIKE SAFETY: AS EASY AS 1-2-3!

1. CHECK YOUR BIKE:

Are your tires firm?

Do your brakes grip?

2. CHECK YOUR BODY:

Wear a bike helmet.

Tie your shoes.

3. CHECK YOUR SURROUNDINGS:

Look both ways before crossing a street.

Watch for road hazards, like potholes or tree branches.

RESPONSIBLE RIDERS ALWAYS:

Obey traffic laws and lights.

Use hand signals when turning.

Say "On your left,"
or ring a bell, when passing.

Ride with a buddy!

WHAT'S YOUR STYLE?

Bell

Streamers

Basket

License Plate

Spoke Beads

Lights

ABOUT THE AUTHOR AND ILLUSTRATOR

LAURA RENAULD is a former elementary school teacher. She lives in Northern Virginia with her husband and their two story-telling sons. She is the author of *Porcupine's Pie* and *Fred's Big Feelings: The Life and Legacy of Mister Rogers*.

JENNIE POH is a creative who studied Fine Art at the Surrey Institute of Art & Design, as well as Fashion Illustration at Central St Martins. She lives in Woking, England.